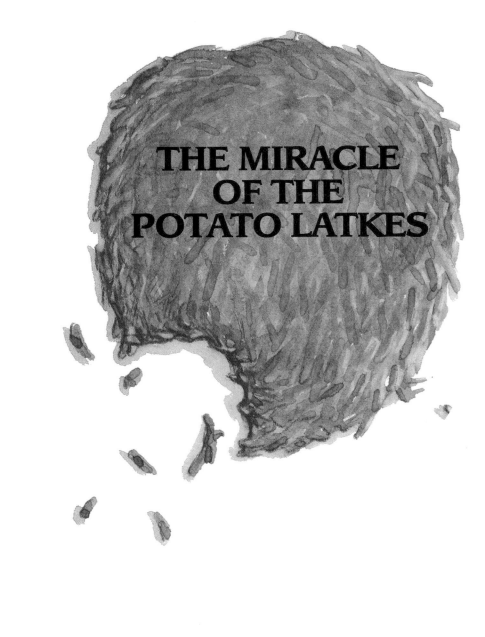

# THE MIRACLE
# OF THE
# POTATO LATKES

Library of Congress Cataloging-in-Publication Data
Penn, Malka.
    The miracle of the potato latkes / Malka Penn ; illustrated by
Giora Carmi. — 1st ed.
        p.   cm.
    Summary: Tante Golda makes the best latkes in all of Russia to
share with her friends at Hanukkah, and even when a poor harvest
leaves her with no potatoes, she is certain that "God will provide."
    ISBN 0-8234-1118-4
    [1. Jews—Russia—Fiction.  2. Hanukkah—Fiction.]  I. Karmi,
Giyora, ill.  II. Title.   93-29921   CIP   AC
PZ7.P38449Mi  1994

# THE MIRACLE OF THE POTATO LATKES

### A Hanukkah Story

## by Malka Penn

## illustrated by Giora Carmi

*Holiday House/New York*

Every year at Hanukkah time, Tante Golda would reach into her wooden barrel and pick out eight of the biggest potatoes she could find. Then she would peel them and grate them and fry them into the most delicious potato latkes in all of Russia.

Her friends and neighbors would crowd into Tante Golda's little kitchen to taste her famous latkes. Tante Golda was never happier than when she stood in front of her black iron stove and cooked batch after batch of golden, crispy latkes and served them to her guests.

"Tante Golda," her guests would say, "these are the most delicious latkes in all of Russia, but you should have saved the potatoes for yourself. There's still a long, cold winter ahead."

"Don't worry about me,"
Tante Golda would smile and say.
"God will provide."

And God did provide. Somehow, Tante Golda's friends and neighbors always managed to drop off a few potatoes now and then, so there was always enough to last her through the winter.

But one year, because of a severe drought, very few potatoes were harvested. When Hanukkah time came around and Tante Golda reached into her wooden barrel, she found only one tiny potato.

"This is terrible!" Tante Golda exclaimed. "Tonight's the first night of Hanukkah—the night I invite all my friends and neighbors over for potato latkes—and I'm down to my last potato!"

She ran next door to her neighbor Risel, to see if she had any extra potatoes.

"I'm sorry, Tante Golda. I don't even have one," Risel said.

So Tante Golda ran down the road to her friend Gittel. But Gittel didn't have any either.

Finally, Tante Golda ran across town to her cousin Hodel, but even Hodel's barrel was empty.

Tante Golda held up her one tiny potato.

"I ask you, Hodel, how can I make a Hanukkah party with one tiny potato?"

"You can't," Hodel said, "unless you're a magician."

"A magician I'm not," Tante Golda sighed.

"Then it will have to be a Hanukkah party without potato latkes," Hodel said.

Hodel's husband, Moishe, looked up from his reading.

"A Hanukkah party without Tante Golda's potato latkes! No one would feel like celebrating."

"I guess you're right," Tante Golda reluctantly agreed. "There can't be a Hanukkah party without potato latkes."

Sadly, Tante Golda trudged home. For the first time that she could remember, there would be no Hanukkah party, no guests filling her house, no golden, crispy latkes.

But as she lit the first Hanukkah candle, and she remembered the ancient miracle of the oil that lasted for eight days, her face brightened.

"God has always provided," she reassured herself. "Maybe God will provide a miracle now."

Just then, there was a knock on the door. An old beggar was standing there, tired and hungry.

"Is this the miracle?" she asked herself. "A beggar wanting food when I hardly have enough for myself?" But of course, she took pity on the poor beggar.

"I was just about to make a potato latke—or two," she told him. "Won't you come in and join me?"

Naturally, the beggar accepted. He entered Tante Golda's small kitchen and bowed.

"Blessings on you, dear lady. I thought tonight I would surely go hungry. But as I always say, 'God will provide.'"

"Oh, do you say that, too?" Tante Golda asked him. "Well then, it must be true. Tonight He's provided me with a guest!"

Tante Golda began peeling and grating her one small potato. She added quite a bit of flour and eggs to stretch the batter, and soon she was frying up a batch of her golden, crispy latkes.

The beggar ate the latkes with great relish.

"These are the best potato latkes in all of Russia," he told her.

"Do you really like them?" Tante Golda asked, pouring him a glass of tea from the samovar.

"Do I like them?" the beggar repeated. "They're delicious! And believe me, it's not just because I'm starving! These latkes nourish body and soul. They are a miracle, and one miracle leads to another. You'll see."

When he finished his tea, the beggar thanked her again and said, "God will surely bless you for sharing your latkes with an old beggar."

After the beggar left, Tante Golda took off her apron and climbed up the steps to her sleeping loft above the stove. She was tired, but happy—almost as happy as if she had made a Hanukkah party for all her friends and neighbors.

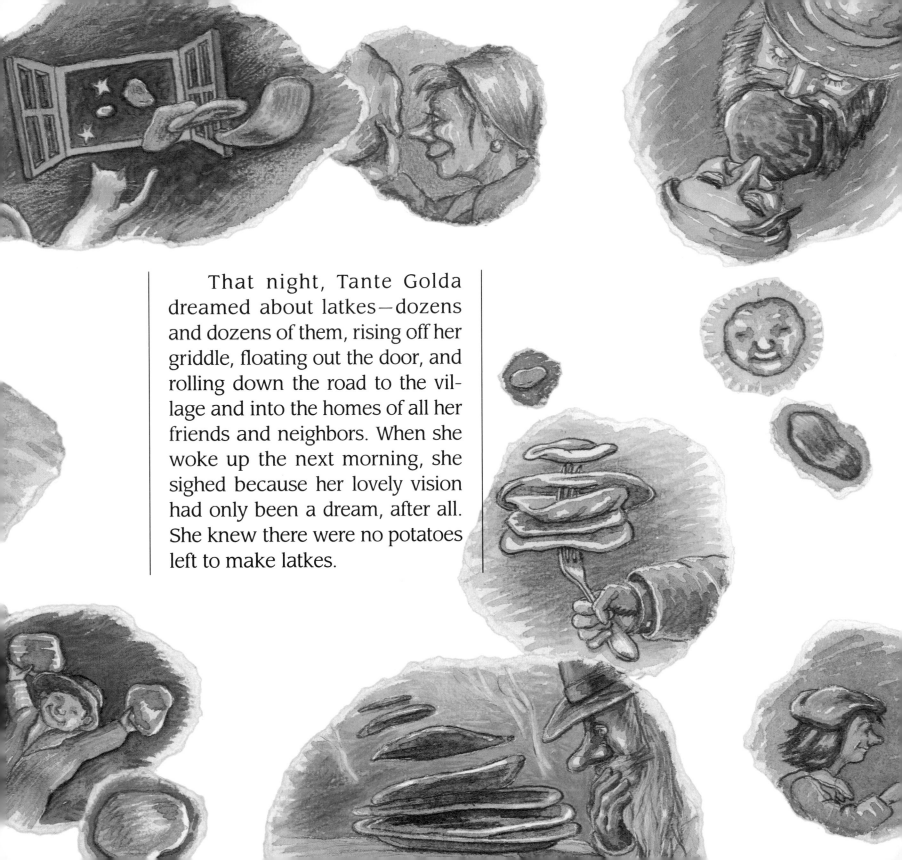

That night, Tante Golda dreamed about latkes—dozens and dozens of them, rising off her griddle, floating out the door, and rolling down the road to the village and into the homes of all her friends and neighbors. When she woke up the next morning, she sighed because her lovely vision had only been a dream, after all. She knew there were no potatoes left to make latkes.

But when she got out of bed, she noticed there were two potatoes sitting next to the menorah.

"Risel must have found some extra potatoes after all," she thought to herself. That night she invited Risel over for a batch of her delicious latkes.

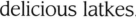

The following day, which was the third day of Hanukkah, Tante Golda woke up and saw three potatoes sitting next to the menorah.

"That Gittel is always trying to fool me," she told herself. "She was just pretending she didn't have any potatoes."

And so it went. Each day Tante Golda woke up, there was one more potato sitting next to the menorah. And each night, she invited one more guest over for latkes.

Finally, on the last day of Hanukkah, there were eight potatoes sitting next to the menorah, and that evening, it was just like it had always been. Eight candles, eight potatoes, eight guests.

Tante Golda stood in front of her black iron stove and cooked batch after batch of her famous latkes.

"These are the most delicious potato latkes in all of Russia," Risel said.

"Not only are they the most delicious latkes," Gittel said, "they're probably the only latkes in all of Russia."

"Tell us, Tante Golda," Hodel asked. "Where did you get the potatoes?"

Moishe winked slyly. "She must be friends with the Czar."

"The Czar, poor man, has never had the good fortune to taste Tante Golda's latkes," Hodel said.

Everyone laughed and helped themselves to another latke.

After they were finished eating, Tante Golda turned to her guests and said, "I know this has been a hard winter for all of us, with very few potatoes to go around. I want to thank you for sharing your few potatoes with me."

"But Tante Golda," her guests said. "Much as we wanted to, we weren't able to give you any potatoes. We had none ourselves."

Tante Golda was surprised, but not too surprised. She remembered the beggar's blessing and knew that somehow, as always, God had provided.

When Tante Golda woke up the next morning, she felt sad as she always did when Hanukkah was over. Perhaps she was even sadder than usual, because now there were no potatoes sitting next to the menorah.

But as Tante Golda got out of bed, she blinked and cried, "It's a miracle!"

There, in the corner, was her wooden barrel, filled to the very top with potatoes. She ran over to the barrel and scooped some potatoes into her hands to make sure she wasn't dreaming. This time, she didn't even try to guess where the potatoes came from. She simply thanked God for providing them.

A barrel full of gold couldn't have made Tante Golda any happier. Now she had potatoes to last until spring, with enough left over to share with her friends and neighbors and cook into batch after batch of golden, crispy latkes.

That year, Tante Golda's Hanukkah lasted all winter long.

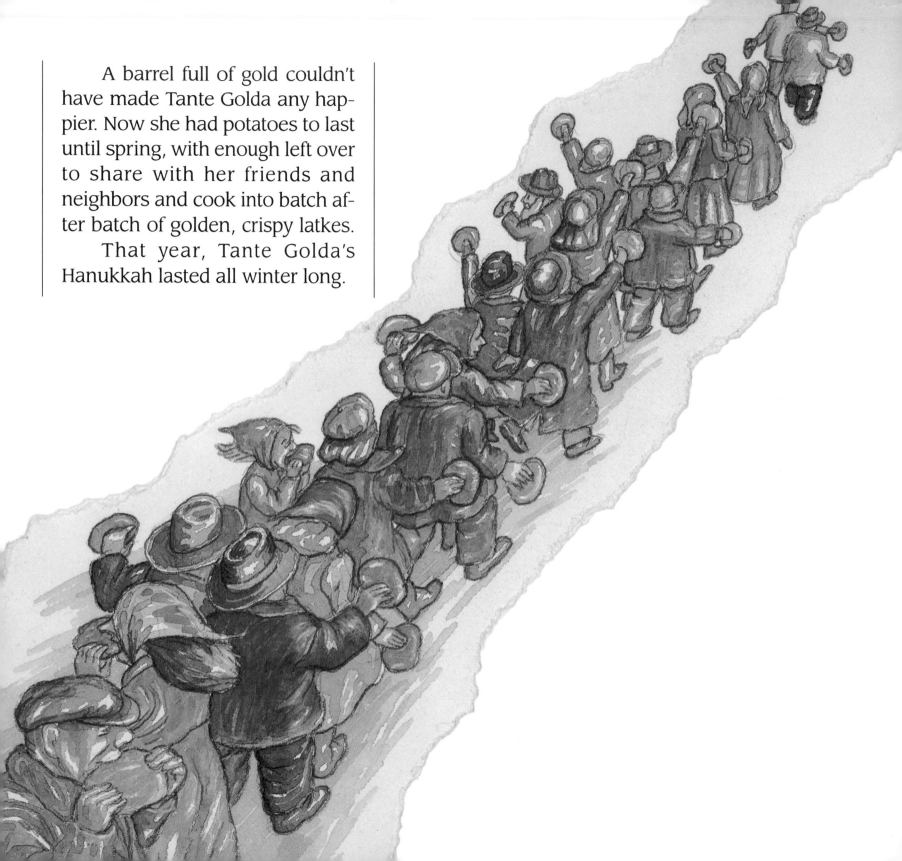

## Tante Golda's Famous Potato Latkes

*(Adult supervision is necessary)*

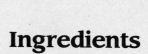

## Ingredients

4 potatoes
1 onion
1 egg
1/2 teaspoon salt
1/4 teaspoon pepper
3 tablespoons flour
1/2 cup vegetable oil

*(go to next page)*

1. Wash the potatoes and peel them. Then grate them and place them in a bowl of cold water. (The water will keep them from turning brown while you're preparing the rest of the recipe.)

2. Peel the onion and chop it into very small pieces.

3. Beat the egg in a large mixing bowl. Add the chopped onion, salt and pepper, and flour.

4. Drain the potatoes in a colander and squeeze the excess water out with your hands. Add the potatoes to the other ingredients and stir until well-blended.

5. Heat half the oil in a skillet over medium heat. Drop the potato mixture in by the tablespoon and cook until browned on both sides.

6. Drain on paper towels. Continue making latkes until the mixture is used up, adding more oil as necessary.

7. Serve warm with applesauce as a topping.

Serves 4–6.